A Dream Come Drew

Written by Carline Dumerlin-Folkes

Illustrated by Lea Embeli

ISBN-13: 978-1981481989

ISBN-10: 1981481982

Dedication

To Andrew, Madison and Rileigh, may
all of your dreams come true.

Bedtime has come once again,

and Little Drew is in his bed.

He is off to sleep, to dream sweet dreams.

Where will his imagination take him?
Let us see!

A city so nice they named it twice;

New York, New York, what a sight!

The Statue of Liberty stands so tall,

and is a symbol to welcome all.

The Brooklyn Bridge allows cars to drive,

way up in the clear blue sky.

Times Square is busy but shines so bright.

No wonder New York is called the City of Lights.

You can ride the subway;
the trains are so fast!

They will get you anywhere in a flash!

And if you need a bite to eat,

a slice of pizza is a treat!

A Broadway Show is just the thing,

to see a cat or lion sing.

There are lots of libraries and museums too.

You can learn about elephants or visit the Central Park Zoo.

There is so much to do in the city that never sleeps,

Just watch out for the taxis — Beep! Beep!

Wow! What a dream!

A Dream Come Drew **Sight Words**

has	so	are
come	they	too
again	it	can
and	what	about
is	up	do
in	blue	never
his	but	out
off	no	for
to	call	a
will	the	of
take	you	see

About the Author

Carline Dumerlin-Folkes is an avid reader whose love for books began at an early age. With many years of experience in the field of education, she is dedicated to helping people develop into their best selves. She is the author of the children's book, *I Will Always Love You* and motivational book, *Kiss the Sky: Reflections on Becoming your Best Self.*

41891396R00018

Made in the USA
Columbia, SC
15 December 2018